ROUTE 40

I0868447

MANISHA M MCCORMACK

ROUTE 40

1ST EDITION FROM THE ONLINE PERSONAL PUBLICATION ON INSTAGRAM

THORPE-BOKER PUBLICATION
ESTABLISHED AUTHOR SOLE TRADER

MANISHA M MCCORMACK

-

For when I am forgetful,
do not let it lead you astray

May you remind yourself —
Of the sweet moments
That you share
With thy self

To you, my true love —
may it be more than a lifetime
on the road

Hopefully, we will see each other
again

-

MANISHA M MCCORMACK

ROUTE 40

MANISHA M MCCORMACK

JUNE 30TH 2027

30

Weighed down
With a deep pit in my chest

As the countdown
comes to a close…

It did not happen
the way it was supposed to be

Now what do I do?
When this pact hadn't come true

JANUARY 16TH 2026

Undercover Pressure

You can’t show that much skin.
You can’t go outside at night.
You can’t be friends with them.
Who knew being born would feel this way?
Mum, I just want to be free…
Mum, I just want to be… me.

MANISHA M MCCORMACK

Autumn 2016

Walking into the an autumn feel
I never thought
That this would be a major time piece.
Hearing my worst fears come to light.
Trying to remind myself why I fell for you.

JANUARY 16TH 2026

Summers

Seeking the floral and perfume
From going on dates
To remembering the days we use to have
Trying to forget
The conversations that would play in my mind

FEBRUARY 2ND 2026

In the Night

Craving you
To move closer in
Sleepless nights
Wearing myself stick thin

MANISHA M MCCORMACK

FEBRUARY 14TH 2026

Nocturnal

Key hidden in the west
Never to find my way
Shadows both follow to the depths

A demon seeking
As the tumbleweed runs over the sand
Will I find you again?
Only, In the morning…

FEBRUARY 18TH 2026

Silver Linings

Lost in a trance
Memorised by your voice
So gentle and clear spoken
I wonder was it right
To say I want a serial killer love?

To be held by you
Will be the death of me
But to loved by you –
Fills the sky
With clouds full of silver linings

Crescent

Similar to a crescent moon
Shedding it’s final phase
I Begin to move forward
To a new beginning

MARCH 10TH 2026

Accidentally in love

Belting your voice
That even the heavens could hear
A smile from side to side
Turning your gaze with a sparkled eye
Reminding me that this love
Is hard to come by

ROUTE 40

MANISHA M MCCORMACK

Middle of the Road

I no longer remember but it was an unusual day and night driving recklessly

MANISHA M MCCORMACK

Voices

Not wanting
To think about you
Yet you're still a topic
To the voices in my head

APRIL 18TH 2026

Lost II

Trying to find
Something new
Looking for words
But all I can remember is you

ROUTE 40

MANISHA M MCCORMACK

MAY 28TH 2026

Lifetime

From a pack of thirty
I found you
Smelling that cigarette
I want you
Holding forth my temptations
I press my lips
Up against you
I hold the flame
Waiting to smell the scent of you

Taste

A rose flavoured smell
As I ignite another
Anguished with a loss
That I cannot recover

JUNE 21ST 2026

Ghost

This time taken away
Has clouded my mind
I'm all out of love
No longer held for time

Can't change my mind,
I've given the space you asked for
I feel good
Now letting go of the ghost of you

FEBRUARY 2ND 2026

Kisses

Kisses from afar
Feelings open like a heavenly door
Treading deep seas
In the hopes you save it all

Woke up
To a thoughtful send
How do I know
There isn’t a nix fuelled end?

JUNE 22ND 2026

Twin Flame

Forwards and backwards
Goes the moving globe
I keep losing my memory
Yet you always remind me of what has happened

I didn't chase you, I ran from you.
I was scared of the connection we share.

You are my twin flame.

It's said time and time again
Your twin is never meant to hurt you

We did
And I still can't recover the time we've lost apart

JUNE 23RD 2026

Pandora's Box

There are always three main characters to this story.
The dynamic trio
Always stuck between living a life they would want
And a life
They are destined to have

Always searching for the box that tells them
What may be best
For the way of life.

One will be destined to open the box.
The other, will be destined to protect the box.
While the fellow
Tried to warn them both to not search for the box at all.

They are simply in a war with themselves
Trying to manage a world that may not love them.

MANISHA M MCCORMACK

JUNE 24TH 2026

Messenger

Do not forget the messenger
for thoughts may deceive you
Trust in the process before you
For time on earth is precious

MANISHA M MCCORMACK

JULY 6TH 2026

Wings

Through the looking glass
you will see a crystal ball
Through the eyes of the beholder
you will shift through the tides

MANISHA M MCCORMACK

In NY

The empire state building
will fall down on a trinket of gold
Flying through the wind
A start of daring times

JULY 7TH 2026

Twisted Fate

Mirroring a bruised sky
She slithers closer to him
Melodies of heavens
Temptress of the sea

As he looks over the edge
Curiosity begins to creep in –
The marine blue waves over
When she beckons him to jump
As he laughs at the ridiculousness
The beauty displayed can't be denied

Removing the clothing that will remain on board
Followed with a dive and a smirked smile
Slowly moving towards his end
A whisper moves through her teeth
Before he could translate
His crimson fate became clear

A sweet exchange between two
To a suffocating death for the new

PROMPT WARNING!

Now

In the Middle of the Road
Wondering how to keep eye contact
Did I stare too hard at those green eyes?
With a hazel stare I smile and grab a blanket behind me
How about I take a turn at driving?

JULY 10TH 2026

Innocent

Some have the luck
To see through the rainbow
Some yell it is a gift
To be able to search
And find the answers that others seek to be found

Some whisper it's a curse
Waking up an innocent
Telling them they are no longer allowed to be silent

Don't say I should fall into the abyss
For what is explained to you
For seeing visions
Is a painful cross to bare

JULY 12TH 2026

Honey Dew

Clear in our minds
Feeling real close to you
As it drips real slow
I push you back
Just to feel you pull me back in
Sticky like honey dew
Flavourful just for you
Wild and unsubdued
Except when your tongue moves through

JULY 17TH 2026

Never

Never did you hear the meaning
Of the words that were meant to show you

Never did you taste the sweetness
Of the nectar that was gifted to you

Never did you smell the animalistic nature
Between our intimate moments

Never did you feel the love
That I would hold just for you

Never did you see me with all eyes
That I would have done anything for you

Never did you sense that I was all in

JULY 5TH 2026

With who?

While I bare
Trying to remind myself
That you are here with me
And not with her

I continue to feed a lie
That will soothe the soft core
Wrapping around my soul

JULY 17TH 2026

Obsession

Sins dressed in different pleasures
Struggling trying to hold
My worldly possessions

A continued obsession
With no real outlook on life

JULY 16TH 2026

Flames

Stuck with your worst habit
Playing a moth to the flame
You continue to alight the ignition
That covers my heart

JULY 16TH 2026

The Fool

Why must you continue to be such a fool?
How did you think it would be okay to toy with me?
Who brought you into the darkness that you so choose to rest in?

When you were clearer
As the skies
Before
The storm

You may see the truth
That you hurt a loving fool
Like a match stick that refuses to light
for that first sweet good morning cigarette

JULY 12TH 2026

Naughty Dates

Pulling you in
With a quick moment away
Filled with dinners
And a good time

JULY 12TH 2026

Women

All the fun we allow ourselves
To hold and let go of
We let our hair down
And our gold trinkets fall
Moving slowly
Closer to our knees

We siren you
To obtain the love we desire
For our actions
Speak louder

JULY 12TH 2026

Dreams

Stuck in a trance
Feeling you close to me
Drifting through air
With no time in our space

MANISHA M MCCORMACK

JULY 25TH 2026

To Constantine

Now don’t forget me –
While you sing to me
Sweet fire left in my soul
With the feeling of you right next to me

JULY 5TH 2026

Losing Me

While I lay bare
Trying to remind myself
That you are here with me
And not with her

I continue to feed a lie
That will soothe
The soft core
That wraps
Around my soul

MANISHA M MCCORMACK

Forbidden Fruit

Was it so bad
To love you?

Now I feel
Forever damned
For eating such a fruit
Disguised with harmful intentions

JUNE 15TH 2026

Seduction

The thought of you lingers —
From my heart
To the nerves that call
Just for you

You seduce me
With your mere sentience
As it lingers
In my nostrils

While my body begins
To feel your soft touches
You pull my hair back
Waking thy higher
In such a heated mess

JULY 25TH 2026

On my knees

Hearing you afar
Beg for my attention
As I beg for yours

JULY 18TH 2026

Northern Lights

Darken Skies
Full of coloured lights
What would secrets do you keep?

Some would drink the juice
Just to know
Others put in the work
Just to see that glow

Filled around nature
It is so bright
You can't help
But feel god's light

MANISHA M MCCORMACK

JULY 18TH 2026

Antarctica – Chilly Night

Charted territories
All divided by treaty marks
Full of snow
All while it burns cold

We continue to dare ourselves
To know
Will we find out during this age?
The treasure you keep

Or will the fauna
From this ice land
Carry on to upkeep
Its ancient secret design
Without ourselves being alive

MANISHA M MCCORMACK

JULY 20TH 2026

Five Leaf Clover

Feeling the breeze
Walking through my hair
Watching blue clouded skies
Dazed with ***Mania*** eyes

Trying to find
A one of a kind
Feeling out of luck
Right in the spring time

Looking down just in time
Stopping for an eye catching surprise
A five leaf clover –

How did all my luck
Rush back
Not sure if it felt fair
But damn, did it feel
Better than air

MANISHA M MCCORMACK

JUNE 1ST 2026

Loving Me

Feeling you
Hold onto me
You wrap your hands around my neck
Taking the soul from me

JULY 22ND 2026

Lost

Similar to a lost man
Trying to get his message across
While stuck in the deep sea
You find yourself losing hope
Just to regain it in yourself

There is beauty in the message
Filled
With either hope or desperation

MANISHA M MCCORMACK

ROUTE 40

MANISHA M MCCORMACK

Route 40

Eating apples
Turbulent winds
Looking over the edge
Violently trying to remain open

Gazing at the ant hill
Viewing the leaves
All attempting
To remain alive and well

Watered Wine

A cup in the air
Wine downed like water
Feeling the heavens
Gift me courage

JULY 27TH 2026

Young

Dying inside
Holding tears at bay
Please remember
You still have a squad would will remember

JULY 29TH 2026

Lost

They are brighter
than the stars in your eyes
Do not forget
What may lead you

JULY 29TH 2026

Sacred Milk

Doesn't it taste delicious
tasting some honey
Missing nothing
as it drips off from the milk fountain

MANISHA M MCCORMACK

Lovely Mind

Trying to let go
of the mania thoughts
leaving us
A sweet taste of nectar
but, alas it was only just —
for a moment

AUGUST 5TH 2026

Thought of you

Distant in the heart
but lost in time
feeling the space grew bigger in between
Will I find the linear year –
Where I am back with you?

MANISHA M MCCORMACK

AUGUST 6TH 2026

Dear Sasha —

Are you sure I am the one you prayed for?
Because I feel like death being caught for things
That I would not want to do.
I miss you, Sasha.

AUGUST 7TH 2026

Timekeepers

Touching the buildings of the city
I cannot help but feel a sense of belonging
Too many questions come through my mind
At the top of the buildings
to the staircases below

MANISHA M MCCORMACK

AUGUST 9TH 2026

Cigarettes

Be careful with it being in the car!
Do not forget to take a piece of me with you
Do not try to upset me in anyway
For I can burn quickly but slowly –
Did you make sure to enjoy
because it has consequences you know

Love,

Mom & Dad

ROUTE 40

After writing the above collection, I slowly was able to recollect myself –
Having CPTSD and with further blocks in memory, I thought to would be best to edit –
and write, about a road on its way to tough times like the older generation before me.

For the readers, may this book bring you lightness and an uplifting feel that I truly desire.
For my love, may you read this back to me when I am lost in two minds.

MANISHA M MCCORMACK

www.ingramcontent.com/pod-product-compliance
Lightning Source LLC
LaVergne TN
LVHW072011300926
849160LV00003B/18
9781764861557